Glastonbury n Bone av Fun wi Flogs

In Black Country Spake

Glastonbury Tails Series

Tim Vincent & Gordon Fanthom

© 2020 by *Tim Vincent & Gordon Fanthom*

All Rights Reserved. No part of this publication may be reproduced in any form or by any means, including scanning, photocopying, or otherwise without prior written permission of the copyright holder.

First Printing, 2020

ISBN: 9798664426793

Dedication

To: Ahn Nuss's n all front line carers n kay grafters werkin fowa ow'm NHS

To: Our Nurses and all front line carers and key workers working for our NHS

Foreword

This book is based on our Children's picture book 'Glastonbury and Bone have fun with Flags'. It is, however, a quite different book in its approach. The story line is written in far greater depth and is told in Black Country dialect. The words written in blue italics at the bottom of each page are an attempted translation of Black Country spake into normal English.

The Black Country is an area of the Midlands, in the UK, where the first coal and iron-based industries developed. The black Country is made up of smaller village type areas, each having their own version of the dialect. This book draws on dialect usage from a lot of these areas. It also includes language examples used by the authors themselves, during their 60 years of life in the region.

It is fine to disagree with our usage of the dialect in the book, but in doing so, you most likely will be greeted by the Tipton chant: 'Ahh day do it, it wore me, yow cor prove it!' Have lots of fun reading this book and maybe try some Black Country spake for yourselves.

Glastonbury n Bone Av Fun wi Flogs

It wore a bad day daahn Millennium Jo's garidge. Glastonbury an Bone was avin a smoshin time playing yed the ball. Meringue Tang yawle'd auht, 'Gizzit ere noggin yed!' The ball drapped from his'n ond. 'Yow caggy onded or summat?' aksed Bone.

It wasn't a bad day down Millennium Jo's Garage. Glastonbury and Bone where having a smashing time playing head the ball. Meringue Tang shouted out, 'Give it here fool!' The ball fell from his hand. 'You left-handed or something?' asked Bone.

'Woss the crack mah mon Bone?' aksed Glastonbury. 'Av yow sid wonn thass on th'ode notice board? The Neverneverton Cahnsul wannt me an yow ter goo daahn thairn meeting ter ark at they'm blabbbrin on about summat,' sed Bone.

'What's going on my man Bone,' asked Glastonbury. 'Have you seen what's on the old notice board? The Neverneverton Council want us to go down to their meeting to listen to them talking about something,' said Bone.

'Woss bin the Neverneverton Cahnsul?' aksed Glastonbury. Bone towd hisn mucka a Cahnsul iss med up of mon and ommon thass tek theer time pitherin abaaht mekin us dun woss weem towd.

'What is the Neverneverton Council,' asked Glastonbury? Bone told his friend a Council is made up of men and women that take their time messing about making us do what we are told.

'Naaaa..,' Glastonbury sed in Kitikat spake. 'Weer Ah bin fram, weem day wannt nah Cahnsuls. Yats dun wass they'm wannt, thas woss the law.'

'Naaa...,' Glastonbury said out loud in Kitikat language. 'Where I come from, we don't need any Councils. Cats do what that they want, that was the Law.'

Aer yats went all rahnd the Reekin ter goo ter Neverneverton in the Grease Monkeys' Octobus sharra. The Panda buz, Hick up truck and Beaky Binder sharra woss theer an'all.

Our cats went the long way round to get to Neverneverton in Grease Monkeys' Octobus. The Panda bus, Hick up truck and the Beaky Binder's people carrier was there as well.

The Cahnsul gaffa, Mayor Dundeal Duck yarle'd aaht at the meeting. Hisn mairt Pig Iron took a sate by Mayor Dundeal Duck who started ter spake in a frenzy an mardy chunter.

The boss of the Council Mayor Dundeal Duck yelled out at the meeting. His friend Pig Iron took a seat by Mayor Dundeal Duck who started to speak in a grumpy and moody voice.

All o' a sudden, Mayor Dundeal Duck went yampy an pukked up hisn wing an Yarle'd aaht, 'Look aaht, summat 'as snuk up an med off wi ow'rn Black Country flog!' E' wass as wicked as a wassp!

Suddenly, Mayor Dundeal Duck went wild and picked up his wing and shouted, 'look! Somebody has thieved our black Country flag!' He was very angry.

Aer crahhd aaht siden Neverneverton gawped. 'Well, Ar'll goo t'the foot o' ooer stairs!' sed Bone. 'Weem think iss the werk of thass feline fiend Scope Yed Muggins!' yowle'd aaht Mayor Dundeal Duck. The crahhd gawped aggen.

The crowd outside Neverneverton gasped. 'I'm shocked!' said Bone. 'We think it is the work of that feline fiend Scope Yed Muggins!' shouted Mayor Dundeal Duck. The crowd gasped again.

Pig Iron spake'd up next. 'This cun turn ockerd. Weem must fun Scope Yed Muggins. E' ud do summat like thass, an we gorra get ahn flog back,' E' sed.

Pig Iron spoke up next. 'This could turn out awkward. We must find Scope Yed Muggins, he would do something like that, and we have got to get our flag back,' he said.

The Cahnsul meeting at Neverneverton ended. Yellow Peg an Stunt Blue weer the fust te fly in ter action. They'm flew up'ards te ger a bostin view.

The Council meeting at Neverneverton ended. Yellow Peg and Stunt Blue were the first to fly into action. They soared upwards to get a good view.

'Tek off now, yow lot! Stondin 'ere ay gerrin the babby washed, am it?' yarled Pig Iron. Theer weer total saftness at Neverneverton as they'm all scattered back'uds to thain sharras.

'Leave right now, you lot. Standing here isn't getting the job done, is it?' shouted Pig Iron. There was total chaos at Neverneverton as everybody scattered and went back to their vans and trucks.

Ow'rn Thai Hares went saft, afta thairn Initiate Master towd they'm te leap in ter action an track daahn Scope Yed Muggins, the suspected flog filcher.

The Thai Hares went wild, after their Initiate Master ordered them to leap into action and track down Scope Yed Muggins, the suspected flag thief.

Afower they'm was gerrin back daahn Millennium Jo's, General Wastrel wass waiting fowa Grease Monkey te put another coot o' wollop on th'ode oss trailer.

Before they got back to Millennium Jo's, General Wastrel was waiting for Grease Monkey to put another coat of paint the old horse trailer.

'A've yow sid tha summat as ad thairn maulers in tha wollop?' yawle'd auht Glastonbury. 'Har, but weege yat med them paw prints?' yawle'd auht Bone.

'Have you seen that something has had their paws in that paint?' shouted Glastonbury. 'Yes, but which cat has made those paw prints?' shouted back Bone.

Glastonbury and Bone went ferritin wi'it to folla the green wollop paw prints. They'm went daahn the cut tow path an dahn past the lime kilns. 'Yow bin fishin daahn this cut afower? aksed Glastonbury. 'Nah, iss jed in theer,' sed Bone.

Glastonbury and Bone went to follow the green paint paw prints. They went down the canal tow path and down past the lime kilns. 'Have you been fishing here before?' asked Glastonbury. 'No, it's dead in there,' said Bone

They'm pukked up the tracks, weege went up a riffy fode by the shap's in the high street. Bone sid tha the Beaky Binders wass just daahn the oss road auht side thairn shap.

They Picked up the tracks, which went up a back alley by the shops in the high street. Bone spotted that the Beaky Binders were just down the road outside their shop.

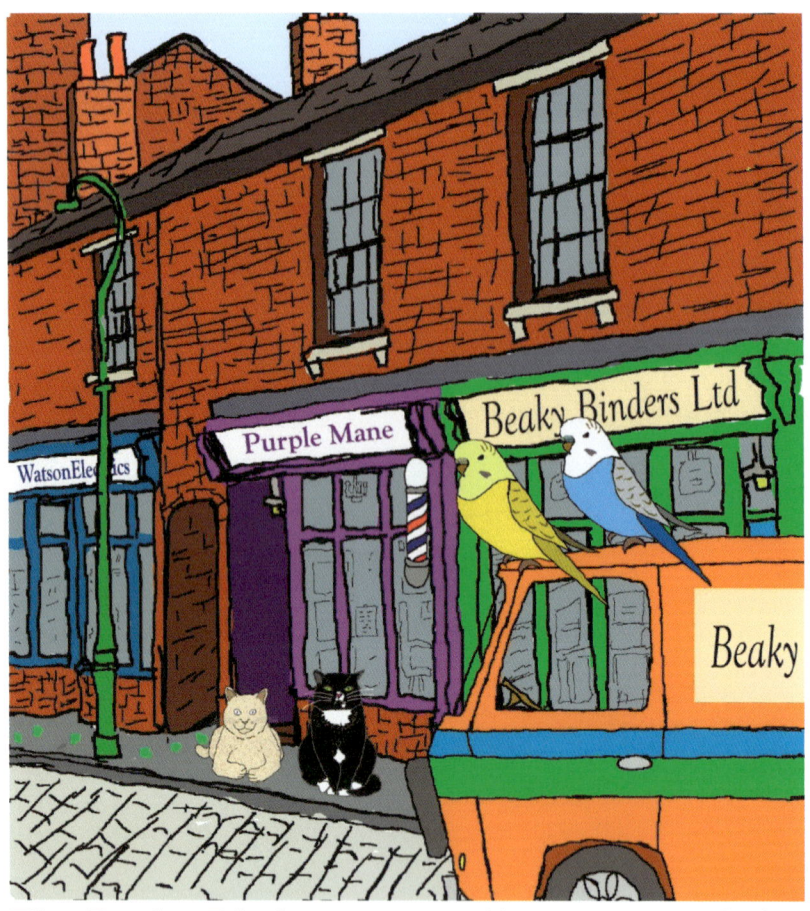

The Beaky Binders wass av'in a sate on thairn ode sharra. Th' yats aksed if they'm had sid or node, weege yat ad med the paw prints? Nayther on um sid owt, they'm yawle'd auht.

The Beaky Binders were having a seat on their bus. The cats asked if they had seen or known which, cat had made the paw prints? Neither of them had seen anything, they chirped out.

'Yow goo daahn in ter the fode an we'ull folla the tracks from up theyer,' sed Stunt Blue. Yellow Peg wass up theer above the fode fust. 'Yow goo in theer fust, Bone,' sed Glastonbury.

'You carry on into the back yard. We'll follow the tracks from above,' said Stunt Blue. Yellow Peg was already flying up over the back yard. 'You go in there first, Bone,' said Glastonbury.

'I sid Scope Yed Muggins,' yarle'd auht Stunt Blue, 'E' snuck out of tha shed by the whimsey.' 'Ah'll goo an get Glastonbury an Bone,' yarle'd back Yellow peg.

'I can see Scope Yed Muggins,' shouted Stunt Blue. 'He's Just coming out of that shed by the pit head.' 'I'll go and get Galastonbury and Bone,' shouted back Yellow Peg.

24

They'm watched in wunda as Scope Yed Muggins snuck up th'ode whimsey. 'Wool thee fly an be gerrin all ow'rn mairts, ull yow. Goo! Goo! Goo!' yarle'd Bone. 'We wow be a jiffy,' yarle'd back the Beaky Binders.

They watched in wonder as Scope Yed Muggins climbed up the old pit head. 'Fly and get our friends will you. Go! Go! Go!' ordered Bone. 'We won't be long,' shouted back the Beaky Binders.

The Beaky Binders day ivver or ovver ter be the fust an tell thair mairt's, an flew rahnd the glassen cone. They'm day av time fer ivverin an ovverin in gerrin hum ter Millennium Jo's.

The Beaky Binders didn't hang around. They wanted to be the first to tell their friends. They flew around the glass cone and then they sped onwards to get home to Millenium Jo's.

When all aar Mairt's ad legged it daahn ter the whimsey at Tacky Bonk Meda, Scope Yed Muggins wass atop the whimsey an began ter unfurl woss sid ter be the Black Country flog e' ad teken.

When all our mates had arrived down at the pit head on Pit Mound Meadow, Scope Yed Muggins was atop the pit head. He began to unfurl what looked like the Black Country flag that he had taken.

Theer wass a gust of wind an suddenly the flog wass flying from the whimsey. Scope Yed Muggins woss well chuffed an began shekin, doncin an loffin. They'm thought e' wass a puddled noggin yed.

There was a gust of wind and suddenly the flag was flying from the pit head. Scope Yed Muggins was happy and began to shake, dance and laugh. The others thought he was nutty.

Mayor Dundeal Duck wass stonding on a green box. E' yarle'd up to Scope Yed Muggins on the whimsey. 'Ger daahn eha roight now an bring daahn ahn flog wi' yow, I woe tell yow aggen, gee it neck!'

Mayor Dundeal Duck stood on a green box. He yelled up to Scope Yed Muggins on the pit head. 'Get down here right now and bring our flag with you. I won't tell you again, give it up!'

'Wass on earth av yow dun t'ow'rn beautiful Black Country flog, yow saft clarnet?' yarle'd Mayor Dundeal Duck in hisen yarle'n voice.

'What on earth have you done to our beautiful Black Country flag, you daft fool?' demanded Mayor Dundeal Duck in a stern voice.

'Ar've bin a workin an dahbed a yat fairce on it, cus ar wanted thuz ter bist a Black Country Yat day,' sed Scope Yed Muggins. 'Yow war very gairn wi' tha wollop, was ya?' sed Pig Iron.

'I've been at work painting a cat face on it, because I wanted there to be a Black Country Cat day,' said Scope Yed Muggins. You aren't very good when it comes to painting, are you?' said Pig Iron.

Glastonbury yarle'd agen ter get in owern Sharra's an ger back to Neverneverton. Scope Yed Muggins an Glastonbury podged in wi Grease Monkey an th'utha's in th' Octobus. 'Ger orf me gammy leg!' yarled Grease Monkey.

Glastonbury shouted out again for us to get into our vehicles and get back to Neverneverton. Scope Yed Muggins and Glastonbury jumped in with Grease Monkey and the others in the Octobus. 'Get off my bad leg!' yelled Grease Monkey.

'Ar wass gooin ter gid it back, Mr Mayor, honest, Ar wass,' sed Scope Yed Muggins as e' wass towd off by the Mayor. E' gid im an order, 'Dow do tharaggen, me mon or yow'll ger a clip rahnd the lug'ole.'

Scope Yed muggings said, 'I was going to bring it back Mr mayor, Honest I was, said Scope Yed Muggins as he was being given a good ticking off by the Mayor. He then gave him an order, 'Don't do it again or you'll get a clip round the ear!'

'Ark,' Peter Panda sed. 'Leave him alone. It ay is fault, an giz ahn kid an new mairt, a fair goo e' ay the fust to dow summat saft. E' wass agooin ter pur it back up a wik after hisn Black Country Yat day.'

'Listen,' Peter Panda said, 'Leave hime alone. It isn't his fault and give our new mate a fair go. He's not the first to do something stupid. He was going to bring it back a week after his Black Country Cat day.'

'Naaaa, ote up a jiffy,' sed Glastonbury. 'I ay gunna shut mar cairk'ole o'er thissen. Hisn Black Country Yat day wore a saft idea, yow kno?'

'Naaa, hold on a minute,' said Glastonbury. 'I'm not going to keep quiet about this one. His Black Country Cat Day wasn't a bad idea, you know?'

'Ar, weem coost ote it on the same day as the Black Country Day!' sed Bone. 'That'n ull do,' they'm all agreed, an nairun voted anunst Black Country Yat Day. They'm all yarle'd 'aaht, 'Bostin!'

'Yea, we could hold it on the same day as the Black Country Day,' said Bone. 'That will be fine,' they all agreed, and nobody voted against Black Country Cat Day. They all shouted out, 'Fantastic!'

'We Thai Hares av owern ohn Black Country flog an yow coost borrow it, till yow gerrin th'utha un back,' sed the Initiate Master. They'm all yarle'd Bostin agen.

'We Thai hares have our own Black Country flag and you are welcome to borrow it until you get the other one back,' said the Initiate Master. They all cheered again.

'I av an idea wonn weem gunna do abaaht it,' sed Mayor Dundeal Duck. E' called over Pig Iron an whispered ter Pig Iron hisn plan on woss ter do abaaht it.

'I have an Idea what we are going to do about it,' said Mayor Dundeal Duck. He called over Pig Iron and whispered to Pig Iron his plan on what to do about it.

38

The very next day Tom Yat Sellbuy cum wi' hisn 'uge Drott. The Mayor towd Tom Yat Sellbuy woon ter do. 'Aweright gaffa, mah mon, iss a piece a cairk,' sed Tom Yat Sellbuy. Pig Iron sed, 'Mind yow dow drap tha omma on sum uns bonce!'

The very next day Tom Cat Sellbuy arrived with his big Drott. The Mayor told Tom Cat Sellbuy what to do. 'Right oh gaffer sir, it's an easy one,' said Tom Cat Sellbuy. Pig Iron said, 'Watch you don't drop that hammer on someone's head!'

Daddy Panda gorrin the Drott's boskit an wass pukked up towards the flogless pole by Tom Yat Sellbuy's Drott. The Beaky Binders flew rahnd an directed woss the crack needed ter be dun up theer, an so they day mek a codge up.

Daddy Panda got in the Drott's basket and was hoisted up towards the flagless pole by Tom Cat Sellbuy's Drott. The Beaky Binders flew around and directed what needed to be done up there, and so they did not make any mistakes.

'It woe be ockerd. From now on we'ull always celebrate Black Country Yats an the Black Country aggen on the same day an'all,' yarle'd the Mayor.

'It won't be difficult. From now on we will always celebrate Black Country Cats and the Black Country again on the same day,' announced the Mayor.

'Hooorah!' they'm yarle'd. 'Naaa ode up mar mon! Weer bist Scope Yed Muggins?' aksed Glastonbury. 'Yow'll fun hisn snuk off hum to tell hisn mairt the keckle witch woss hisn bid a dun,' sed Bone 'Dow werrit he'ull be gerrin back, e' always cums back.'

'Hooorah!' they cheered.' Naaa, wait my friend! Where's Scope Yed Muggins?' asked Glastonbury. 'I think you will find he has gone home to tell his friend the Kettle witch what he has been doing,' said Bone. 'Don't worry, he'll be back as always.'

The Cast

The Yats played by:
Glastonbury
Bone

The Filcher played by:
Scope Yed Muggings

The Pandas played by:
Amanda Panda
Peter Panda
Krishy Panda

The Beaky Binders played by:
Stunt Blue
Yellow Peg

The Cahnsul Mayor played by:
Mayor Dundeal Duck

The Cahnsul Clerk played by:
Pig Iron

The Thai Hares played by:
Initiate Master
Captain Leebay
Cash O' Carry

Oss race champion played by:
General Wastrel

The Grease Monkeys played by:
Grease Monkey
Meringue Tang
Grease Tang

Hot's to Drott's operator played by:
Tom Yat Sellbuy

Tararabit

The End

Download the Glastonbury song from:
http://timvincentauthor.co.uk/glastonbury-tails/

Get your copy of the first book in the Glastonbury Tails series from Amazon. Use this link: https://amzn.to/2OnZ4qa

Printed in Great Britain
by Amazon